D1077322

Text copyright © 1999 Anthony Masters
Illustrations copyright © 1999 Alan Marks

First published in Great Britain in 1996
by Macdonald Young Books Ltd

This edition re-issued in 2008 by Wayland

All rights reserved

The right of Anthony Masters to be identified as the author of this Work and the right of Alan Marks to be identified as the illustrator of this Work has been asserted by them in accordance with Copyright, Designs and Patents Act 1988

This book is sold subject to the condition that it shall not, by way of trade or otherwise, be lent, re-sold, hired out, or otherwise circulated without the publisher's prior consent in any form of binding or cover other than that in which it is published and without a similar condition including this condition being imposed on the subsequent purchaser.

Printed in China

British Library Cataloguing in Publication Data available

ISBN: 978 0 7502 5410 6

Wayland is a division of Hachette Children's Books,
an Hachette Livre UK Company
www.hachettelivre.co.uk

THE GHOST BUS

ANTHONY MARKS

Illustrated by Alan Marks

WAYLAND

COVENTRY SCHOOLS LIBRARY SERVICE	
30-Jan-2009	JF
PETERS	

Chapter One

The river was flowing so fast that Jack and Tina were sure it would burst its banks at any moment. Uprooted bushes and small trees, a plastic dustbin, wooden fencing and a road sign were being hurled along by the ferocious current.

Watching from the other side of the road they were afraid and excited at the same time.

The river was so angry, so violent. They
had never seen such a fierce torrent
before, but Dad had
told them that

twenty years ago it had actually burst its
banks. A boy, who had foolishly been
fishing in the raging water, was almost

swept away and drowned. Fortunately, the driver of a passing bus had climbed on to the broad trunk of a fallen oak tree and managed to drag him to safety.

"The old oak tree's still there," said Jack. "But the water's so high you can only just see it."

The river was making a deep roaring sound. The boiling surface was a muddy swirling brown colour, and spray was rising as the waves hit the banks with a horrible tearing, gulping noise.

"If it does flood we won't have to go to school," said Tina. "Then we'll miss the maths test."

"Suppose the water comes into the house?" Even the

thought of missing a maths test didn't comfort Jack.

"Come in at once!" yelled their mother, standing on the front step. "It's dangerous out there."

The light outside was fading fast as Jack and Tina took a last look at the angry river. Its roaring sound seemed louder, but now they could hear something else – a kind of sighing that stayed in their ears and refused to go away.

"What is it? The wind?" asked Tina, but Jack didn't hear.

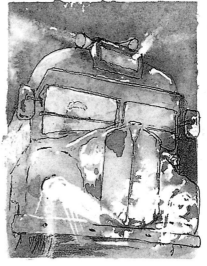

The blasting of a horn echoed and re-echoed as a single-decker bus came into view, driving fast. Despite the deepening twilight, it had a strange shimmer. The bus was old fashioned, and had EXTRA SERVICE on its blind. Tina and Jack stared at it unbelievingly, a terrible chill gripping their stomachs, filling both of them with a fear that was far greater than the hurtling river.

Then they caught a glimpse of the driver, bent over the wheel.

"I saw through him, I'm sure I did," muttered Jack.

Tina gazed intently at the retreating misty figure. Her brother had been right.

Then the bus vanished and they were left shivering. The flooding river was easier to cope with because it was real. The bus wasn't.

Chapter Two

Mum yawned as they all sat round the
scrubbed pine table having supper. She'd
had a hard day at the office.

"You kids look pale," said Dad, cutting
up a beefburger hungrily. "You don't think
you've picked up the 'flu, do you?"

"They can't miss the maths exam," said
Mum in her spoilsport voice.

"I do feel a bit feverish," said Jack, seizing the opportunity.

Mum came over and felt their foreheads. "Nothing wrong at all," she said briskly. "Clear these plates away and get on with your homework."

That night Jack dreamt he was crawling along the fallen oak tree, trying to grab a hand that was just out of reach.

Below him, a boy of about his own age was clinging to a tree root, but the current was trying to pull him away.

"Reach up!" Jack yelled.

"I can't!"

"You must!" Jack tried to flatten himself on the trunk, but it was cold and wet and slippery and he was terrified he might fall in.

A great wave of freezing cold water surged up, soaking him, pulling at him with incredible force.

Then he was in the river, being carried along at a terrifying speed. Suddenly, above the booming flood-stream, he heard the echoing of a horn. Curiously, he wasn't afraid this time; the sound was almost comforting.

As Tina and Jack stood by the bus stop next morning, he told her about his dream.

"That's weird," she said. "I had exactly the same one."

They stared at each other in horrified amazement. This had never happened before.

"You heard the echoing horn?" he asked.

"Yes, I know I did."

"What does it mean? Was that a ghost bus we saw last night?"

Chapter Three

The test had been hard, and Tina was so
tired that she had fallen asleep at her desk
and had to be woken up by a furious Mrs
Stevens.

She gave her famous bared-teeth smile.
"Tina – see me at break."

"She gave me a detention," Tina told
her brother in the playground. "Said I'd

been sitting up late
watching TV. So
don't bother to
wait for me after
school. Old Stevens
has already phoned
Mum at the office.

I'll get home on my own." Tina gulped
and Jack knew she was close to tears.

"Of course I'll wait for you," he said
fiercely.

The rain was bucketing down again as
they waited alone at the bus stop outside
the school gates.

"Do you reckon the water will get in the house?" Jack asked anxiously.

"Maybe," Tina replied, yawning. All she wanted was her bed – even if it was afloat.

"We could write up the story and sell it to the papers," said Jack.

"Write it up?" gasped Tina. "That reminds me – I've left my maths book behind and the caretaker's locked the gates."

Seeing the street was empty, Tina began to climb the gates.

"Hang on. I'm coming with you," said Jack loyally.

Luckily their classroom was unlocked; even more luckily there was no sign of the caretaker. Tina found  her maths book and they scrambled back unseen.

Then she looked at her watch and groaned. "We've missed the bus and the next one isn't till half past. We've got ages..."

But Jack was gripping her arm.

"What's up? You're hurting!"

"I thought I heard something."

The rain was only spitting now and a mist was closing in. Dimly they heard the echoing horn.

The sighing began as the bus swept round the corner with its EXTRA SERVICE sign on the blind.

Through the steamed-up windows they could just make out the passengers and the driver.

"I can see through all of them," gasped Tina.

"You're dead right," Jack replied, and his voice shook as he repeated the word 'dead'.

Slowly, the automatic door opened to complete silence. No running of an engine, no sound of people talking. Just silence.

Tina shrank back. "Let's walk home," she said. "I don't care how long it takes."

"Good idea." But as Jack spoke a rush of cold, damp air seemed to billow out of the interior of the bus, drawing them up the steps, towards the blank staring eyes of the see-through passengers.

Chapter Four

Much to Tina's amazement, Jack automatically showed his bus pass to the wraith-like driver, but the driver gazed straight ahead, and didn't even glance at them. Then they both turned back to the ghostly passengers, all of whom wore outdated clothes and had pale, wide-open eyes that were fixed on Jack and Tina in deadly concentration as they slowly and uneasily sat down.

Jack began to shake violently. Their eyes were boring into him, their grey cracked lips parted in chilling smiles.

Tina jumped up as Jack suddenly ran back to the door, but it wouldn't open. "We got on the wrong bus, let us out!" she yelled, but the driver just stared ahead. Then the sighing began again and the bus started to move.

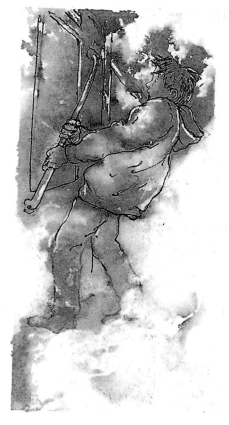

Returning fearfully to their misty seats, Jack and Tina knew they were trapped. They were sitting amongst the dead.

Panicking, Jack got to his feet again and began to pull frantically at the emergency handle,  but it wouldn't budge. A horrible smell of damp earth seemed to surround him and he screamed as he felt the clutch of an ice-cold hand. Whimpering with fear he stared down to see a young woman pulling at his anorak with her transparent bony fingers.

"You're needed," she whispered, as if from a long distance away. "You can't leave now."

The bus was picking up even more speed as the rain poured down outside. Yet there was a deep silence and they couldn't hear anything except the sighing and sometimes the echoing horn.

"It's like being under water," stuttered Jack.

"More like under the ground," replied Tina.

The cold was getting worse and they could feel it penetrating their bones.

The bus began to slow down as it neared the river and then came to a halt, its engine ticking over, the ghostly passengers staring ahead.

Slowly the driver got up and turned towards them, staring from the deep, dark sockets of his eyes.

"Can you open the door please?" Jack's voice shook.

The driver began to walk silently down the aisle towards them.

"The door," said Tina. "Please can you open the door? This is where we get off."

The driver stopped beside them, his chalk-white face staring at them intently, the earthy smell very strong.

"You're needed," he whispered distantly.
"I can't reach him. Not now."

"I don't know what you're on about,"
said Jack.

"Look through the window and you'll
find out," whispered Tina.

Chapter Five

They could just make out the boy in the river, clutching desperately at the bank, the flood lashing and tearing at his outstretched arms.

The door of the bus silently slid open and Jack and Tina could hear the rain again, the roaring of the water, and the faint cries for help.

Jack shouted, "Hold on! We're coming. Don't let go!" But he couldn't hear any answering cry.

Jack and Tina could see the river was at last beginning to burst its banks. Although they were both strong swimmers they knew they would stand no chance in the hurtling stream. Its roaring seemed to have become a growl and the horror of the ghost bus was replaced by the thrusting menace of the river.

"Hold on!" yelled Jack to the boy.

"I can't," he gasped.

"You've got to," said Tina. "You can't let go now."

But just as she spoke he lost his grip.

The current grabbed him, whirling the boy towards the centre of the river. He struck out, swam a couple of metres and managed to grab an overhanging branch of the fallen oak tree. But it was almost

submerged now and Jack and Tina could hardly hear themselves shout over the thundering roar.

"I'm heavier than you!" yelled Jack. "I'll get out on the trunk."

"I'll hang on to your ankles," Tina replied.

Without hesitating they ran towards the dark water which was beginning to overflow the banks with a horrible sucking sound.

Jack slid along the wet trunk, wrapping his legs round it, grabbing at dead branches. One snapped off and he would have fallen in if Tina hadn't steadied him from behind.

"I can't hold on much longer!" yelled the boy.

"Almost with you." Jack knew he had to sound more confident than he felt. "What's your name?"

"Sam."

As he spoke, Jack and Tina heard the echoing horn of the ghost bus. But this time, as in their dream, it was more comforting than threatening and seemed to give them strength.

Jack was struggling forward on his stomach now, but was almost swept off as the cold grey-green water rushed over him. Tina grabbed her brother's ankles and gradually he drew alongside Sam, whose teeth were chattering. His hands, locked around the branch, were blue.

"When I lean over, grab me round the neck," Jack commanded.

Sam let go of the branch but then grabbed it again. The river continued to thunder past, wrenching at Sam's arms and legs. Jack knew that if his limbs went numb like Sam's, he would soon slip into the freezing water.

"I'll count to three – and then you grab me!" he yelled.

The echoing horn sounded again and again and another burst of strength seemed to fill Jack as the river roared louder and even more threateningly.

Chapter Six

"One. Two."

Jack leant over as far as he could, and Tina, her knees biting tightly into the slippery tree trunk, took the strain on his ankles.

"Three."

Sam reached up and grabbed Jack's neck in a vice-like grip with his slimy, freezing fingers.

"Climb over me."

The bus's echoing horn kept sounding as the three of them fought the river.

Then, with a last effort, Sam hauled himself up, put his feet on another branch of the dead oak tree, let go of Jack's neck and grabbed him round the waist.

Sam's heavy,
waterlogged boots
caught Tina in the
stomach, and she
gasped as he inched
his way to safety.

Jack struggled
into a sitting
position and he and
his sister slid back along the slippery
trunk.

As they stumbled over the wet grass, Jack and Tina could see the bus driver's dark eyes staring out of his cab. His dead

lips were parted in a smile and the transparent passengers gazed from the shadowy windows in triumph.

The ghost bus sighed, and with a final blast of its echoing horn began to glide silently up the hill.

As it disappeared into the mist, Jack and Tina were sure they could hear the sound of ghostly applause.

"What are you staring at?" demanded the shivering Sam. "Did I hear a horn? It was kind of…"

"Where do you live?" interrupted Tina.

"We just moved into that cottage over there. I was looking for my dog, Champ." Sam's voice faltered. "I wondered if he'd been swept away and I went down to the river to look. Then I got a bit too close."

"There's your dog," said Tina as a small terrier ran up, licking Sam's wet face.

Jack watched the ghost bus suddenly break through the gloom as it crested the hill.

Champ was playing with something on the ground, barking and worrying at it ferociously.

"He's got a bus ticket," said Sam, picking it up. "But it looks old fashioned. How strange, it must have been here for years."

Jack and Tina knew that it hadn't.

DARE TO BE SCARED!

Are you brave enough to try more titles in the Tremors series? They're guaranteed to chill your spine...

The Curse of the Ghost Horse by Anthony Masters
Jake believes the ghost tale of Black Bess, a horse that fell to her death when forced to jump a huge crevasse. He is convinced the ghost horse is cursing his family and is determined to jump the crevasse to find Black Bess. But will Jake's obsession lead to his death...?

The Headmaster's Ghost by Sam Godwin
It's the school trip to Mortimer Hall. Adam and Melissa decide to scare Danny senseless by telling him the story of the evil headmaster's ghost who haunts the house. Danny is determined to show he isn't scared. But does his detemination bring him more than he bargained for...?

Time Flies by Mary Hooper
When Lucy hides in the wooden chest at the old manor house, it's just a game. But then she gets the fright of her life when she opens the lid and discovers that everything has changed. Somehow she has gone back to Tudor times and now she's trapped in a strange and terrifying world...

All these books and many more in the Tremors series can be purchased from: *The Sales Department, Hachette Children's Books, 338 Euston Road, London NW1 3BH.*

3 8002 01665 6599

Hi Lo